The Library
Lambeth Colle
Vauxhall Cenu
Wandsworth R
London
SW8 2JY

GW00720619

# Funny What Smells Can Do

## Kathleen Claffey

LAMBETH COLLEGE LIBRARIES

3 8073 00063 7564

GR CLA
0637564
6/06

Text copyright © Kathleen Claffey & Gatehouse Books Ltd 2004
Illustrations, Heather Dickinson
Cover photograph, Anne Chester
Editor, Anne Chester
Published and distributed by Gatehouse Books Ltd.
Hulme Adult Education Centre, Stretford Road, Manchester M15 5FQ
Printed by RAP Ltd., Oldham.
ISBN 1 84231 010 0
British Library cataloguing in publication data:
A catalogue record for this book is available from the British Library

This writing was originated and developed in the course of the Gatehouse "New
Readers New Writers Roadshow" project with funding from the Royal Mail Group's
Stepping Stone Fund.

Many thanks to the New Readers New Writers Roadshow Reading Circle: Z. &
Y.Affridi, J.Barker, C.Barrow, D.Blake, B.Farrell, S.Fitzpatrick, J.S.Forrest, L.Green,
J.Garvey, C.Hokat, B.Lake, B.Lucy, P.Martin, J.McKenzie, C.Morrison, S.Naznin,
D.Quinton, A.Roscoe, S.Ryan, A.Simpson, M.Taylor, M.Tetteh-Lartey, M.Toohill,
F.Wallwork, H.Williams, M.Wells.

Many thanks for their support, kindness and encouragement to Peter Harrison and
Steph Prior.

Gatehouse is grateful for continued financial support from Manchester City Council,
and for financial assistance from the Royal Mail Group's Stepping Stone Fund for the
development of this publication.

Our thanks for their ongoing support to Manchester Adult Education Service.

Gatehouse is a member of The Federation of Worker Writers & Community
Publishers.
Gatehouse Publishing Charity is a charity registered in England no. 1011042.

Gatehouse provides an opportunity for writers to express their thoughts and feelings
on aspects of their lives.
The views expressed are not necessarily those of Gatehouse.

My favourite food as a child,
especially in the winter,
was baked rice pudding.

I would get the smell
as I got to the front gate.
How cosy, to come in out of the cold
into that nice warm kitchen,

and the warm pungent smell
of cinnamon and sultanas,
the burnt smell of the milk
that had formed a brown, crispy skin
over the rice.

My mother cooked the pudding
in a big, cream, enamel pie dish.

I would be first
to sit at the table
with my spoon.
Me and my brothers would fight
over the scraping of the dish
when it was empty.

If I won the dish
I would spend hours
just scraping around the sides.

Now that I am grown up
I cook my own baked rice,
but it never turns out
just as nice
as my mum's.

It has now become
an old fashioned dish
and it's seldom on the menu

but if ever I do see it on the menu

I will order it,

hoping I am going to get

that certain taste,

and let it roll all around my mouth,
letting the taste buds jump
in pure delight.
Mmm ..... lovely!

# About the Author

By the grace of God I write this introduction.
I have no doubt in my mind
it is a miracle.
When I was a carer,
it was difficult for me to write a shopping list.
It was hard to know the first letter of a word to write.
Taking a pen in my hand would start the burning
and the sweat down my back.
I would rather have dug a ditch than try and write.

Twice in my life
I have been wrote off as a hopeless case.
First as a child
and later as an adult.
Now I am writing an introduction.
You might think it's a small book.
To me it's a beautiful, big, big book.

I am so glad I was persuaded to go to classes
at Cedar Mount Adult Education Centre.
I was given one to one dyslexia support.

I hope you enjoy this book
I would love everyone to know
that it's never too late to learn.
Now I know why the pen is mightier than the sword.

*Kathleen Claffey*

# Gatehouse Books

**Gatehouse is a unique publisher**
Our writers are adults who are developing their basic
reading and writing skills. Their ideas and experiences
make fascinating material for any reader, but are
particularly relevant for adults working on their reading
and writing skills. The writing strikes a chord - a shared
experience of struggling against many odds.

The format of our books is clear and uncluttered. The
language is familiar and the text is often line-broken, so
that each line ends at a natural pause.

Gatehouse books are both popular and respected within
Adult Basic Education throughout the English speaking
world. They are also a valuable resource within
secondary schools, Social Services and within the Prison
Education Service and Probation Services.

# Booklist available

Gatehouse Books
Hulme Adult Education Centre
Stretford Road
Manchester
M15 5FQ
Tel/Fax: 0161 226 7152
E-mail: office@gatehousebooks.org.uk
Website: www.gatehousebooks.org.uk

The Gatehouse Publishing Charity Ltd is a registered charity, no. 1011042
Gatehouse Books Ltd is a company limited by guarantee, reg no. 2619614